Anita Mulvey had always dreamed of being a writer although it wasn't until something strange happened that she was finally able to begin writing in earnest. In April 2018, Anita suddenly went blind and eventually retired from primary school teaching, a job she loved. But this unexpected event enabled her to embark on her journey to become an author. Anita says that positive outcomes can occur even when we are faced with adversity – never give up hope!

Born and raised in Aldershot, Hampshire, Anita now lives very happily on the beautiful Isle of Man.

New Website
anitamulvey.com

Dedicated to my fantastic parents, Sandra and Ian, with thanks for all their support and encouragement.

Anita Mulvey

THE CORONA CHRONICLES

AUSTIN MACAULEY PUBLISHERS®

LONDON * CAMBRIDGE * NEW YORK * SHARJAH

A CIP catalogue record for this title is available from the British Library.

ISBN 9781035843190 (Paperback)
ISBN 9781035843206 (ePub e-book)

www.austinmacauley.com

First Published 2025
Austin Macauley Publishers Ltd®
1 Canada Square
Canary Wharf
London
E14 5AA

Thanks to:

Sight Matters (also known as Manx Blind Welfare) for all their support, training and technology.

All the super staff at St. Paul's Eye Hospital, Liverpool, for their continuing care.

My wonderful family and friends, with special mention to my partner, Dave, for his help with paperwork.

All the children I have ever taught – thanks to you all for teaching me!

Finally, all the fabulous people at Austin Macauley Publishers who are helping me to fulfil my dreams.

Prologue

Dear Justine & Raquel,

Only time for a quick e-mail as we're dashing over to my mum's flat. We've decided that she should move into our spare room as we are almost certainly going into lockdown next week. Seems the best option for us all and she won't be isolated – such strange times this Corona Virus pandemic has brought us to!

And I've set up a Friendship Forum so that we can all post our thoughts, worries, diaries – whatever! So much better than a round robin of e-mails, I thought. We can keep in touch and support each other all from the comfort of our – er – "locked-down" homes – what do you think? After all, we're not going to be able to meet up for, well, who knows how long?!

Hope you like my idea – and don't mind that I've already asked my former neighbour to join the forum (she's called Lois and she's been rather isolated already since her husband died a few years ago).

Must dash – have a fantastic last weekend of freedom! Lots of love, Amy xxx

Hello, dear friends,

Here is my first instalment for our new forum. Hope that you all find time to add yours too – it will be fun to keep up to date during these restricted times of lockdown. I look forward to reading your news soon. Stay positive and safe!

Prepare to be amazed – hopefully, I'm going to get a bit fitter at last! Read on for the explanation of my most uncharacteristic behaviour!

We've all heard so much about global warming and the other environmental issues, haven't we? I agree that humans are putting our planet in danger and I'm determined to do my bit. After all, I have two wonderful children and I want to help ensure that they have a great future, along with any children they may have one day. You could say that I have a vested interest in trying to reduce my own carbon footprint.

But where should I start?

I think that my car is the obvious concern. When I first purchased it, I'd been so pleased with its unleaded fuel consumption and catalytic-converter – whatever that is! So I had a "green" car which was better for the environment, or so I thought at the time.

But now they are planning to do away with these types of car because they are considered to be bad for the environment. Now the talk is all about electric cars. Yes, I do see the point of these, leaving aside all the worries over recharging – but I simply can't afford to buy a new car.

So I've decided to buy a bicycle. I've not ridden a bike for over 20 years, but that shouldn't be a problem, should it?

My proud new cycle is red and shiny, rather like a famous but unecological racing car. I've got a brilliant-red safety helmet and matching cycle gloves. So I'm all set to go.

But my children are decidedly unimpressed. They've got used to "Mum's taxi" ferrying them everywhere. I've told them that it's much healthier for us all to walk to school, me pushing my new bike, ready to cycle onwards to work. But they complain that their school bags are too heavy and ask what will happen on the many rainy days. I struggled along yesterday on the first morning of our new regime, with Julie's bag over one shoulder, my own rucksack over the other shoulder and Mark's bag dangling from my handlebars. Nightmare!

And both my offspring were decidedly embarrassed to be seen with me wearing my new helmet – but I simply couldn't carry anything else!

At the school gates they grabbed their bags and vanished into the playground, refusing my usual goodbye kiss. They ran together to the far end of the school yard, and I just know that they were both praying that none of their friends had seen them with me!

As you may recall, my mother always collects them after school – in her non-electric powered gas-guzzling monster – so there were no issues for my children there. But my intended review of their school bags and whether they really needed everything every day was rendered quite redundant. Both my little rascals had arranged to be picked up this morning by their friends and driven to school in their accustomed style. Clever Julie has even organised a rota for her friends and their accommodating parents.

Well, that does make my life a bit easier. But I have to confess that I absolutely hate cycling to work! It's not too bad on the new cycle lanes, but I still get unnerved when large or noisy vehicles go past me. You might not think so, but buses and lorries are quite scary!

Well, I've only had two days of cycling so far. Fingers crossed that I'll soon get used to it, as my dear old car gathers dust on our drive! That's all for today – new instalment soon! Have a great week,

Love Amy xxx

Hello everyone,

Many thanks to Amy for setting up this forum. I am so excited to hear how you are all getting on – even though I do feel rather guilty somehow, when we are lucky enough to be out of our "circuit-breaker" lockdown here on this beautiful, little island while you are all still coping with the restrictions. Nevertheless, do read on please for my first instalment!

Today began very blustery with a forecast of rain. I hoped that it would stay fine for at least the first hour or so, as I drove to my only appointment of the day (most shops, etc. are open but business is decidedly slow).

As I unlocked the front door to show my clients around the house for sale, I extolled its virtues: the door was both sturdy and original, really setting the scene for this attractive, period cottage. My point was somewhat negated as I had to raise my voice to cover the ominous creaking of the ancient hinges.

As we stepped indoors, I announced in my best "estate agent-speak" that the hallway was truly magnificent. I chuntered on about the beautiful, Victorian tiles being much sought-after, but neither viewer saw fit to comment.

I drew their attention to the decorative coving and the deep skirting boards, remarking that no-one could fail to be impressed by the ornate ceiling in the first reception room.

The woman's reply was simply a non-committal murmur whilst her husband gave a loud snort of derision.

Taking no notice I breezed on into the next room, trying to set the scene for the super soirées they could have in this "Drawing Room" or "Withdrawing Room" to give it its formal title.

My valiant efforts were rewarded with the man's muttering of "soirées indeed!" just loud enough for me to hear. Some clients are harder work than others!

I pressed on to the room across the hallway, ignoring his rudeness as I praised the marvellous fireplace and over-mantle in the second reception room.

But of course these difficult viewers did not agree. They commented on how dark the room was, stating that it needed a total re-vamp and several coats of magnolia to drag this black hole into the 21st century!

Well, I am sad to say that it all went downhill from there. The final nail in this house's coffin went in as we all trooped up the stairs. At the exact moment that we stepped into the "deceptively-spacious" landing, the skies darkened and the rain fell in torrents. Large drops of water splashed on us as simultaneously we all gazed up at the ceiling. Even my 17 years as an estate agent could provide me with nothing positive to say about a roof which leaked like a sieve.

My clients naturally had lots to say, but they weren't positive either. With declarations that the roof would cost a fortune to replace with all the scaffolding needed, the horrid husband said that no re-vamp would sort out this house of horrors; rather it needed knocking down and re-building completely. As he started down the stairs, his equally unpleasant wife saw fit to remark that they had seen quite enough of this dump!

What could I say? Nothing! They did have a fair point. But the sad thing is that the house really could be wonderful – if the new owners had imagination and perhaps a rather large bank balance.

Caffeine was definitely needed after that encounter!

Back at my office, we decided that the cute bird name of this house's road should be re-named. The suggestions varied from Dodo, to Albatross to Dead Duck – what do you all think?

I hope very much that your day has gone better than mine! Love to you all, Justine x

Greetings to you all,

I hope that you're all well. I think the forum is a great idea although I'm not sure that you'll be much interested in my meagre offerings. It's so difficult to find much to write about as we're shielding because of Daisy's heart problems. Lockdown for us means that most days are so similar. Perhaps we should all take up Japanese or pottery or whatever? Maybe it would be like that film where the main character has to repeat every day, learning to become a fabulous piano player along the way?

What can I tell you? I'm sure that there are many people in worse positions than me, but lockdown isn't easy in a tiny flat with two nine-year-old children and no access to a garden!

I've decided that all three of us need to find one positive every day to combat any negatives.

Today my biggest negative was my resolve to not snack between meals. The gloomy day had me wavering before the morning was even half-way through! As the twins argued over the laptop, I decided on just one chocolate biscuit and an extra-large cup of tea.

However, the kids began fighting over the television and my willpower crumbled completely. Three biscuits later, I looked out of the window and saw the most fantastic rainbow – it really made my day. The kids loved it too and it inspired them to draw it. I was pleased with both pictures and they are now in pride of place on our noticeboard in the kitchen.

By the way, I tried to remember that old rhyme to help people remember the sequence of colours in rainbows. I had to look it up online in the end – but my delightful darlings weren't particularly interested anyway…

It really has been one of those days!

Love to you all, Raquel x

Hello again, dear friends,

It was great to read your news and I hope that you all feel more connected with this new forum – I certainly do!

I've had quite a good week and thank our lucky stars that my mother lives with us now. Things would be so difficult if she wasn't a member of our household, with both Andy and I being classed as "key workers". But I've discovered that being passed by other traffic is not the worst thing about cycling. Do read on for this week's news!

Worst of all about cycling is that I arrive at work looking an absolute wreck! Even after a whole week, the situation hasn't improved. Cycling makes me so hot that I really need a shower when I get to my school – but then I worry that I would not be saving the environment much if I have to use up more power to heat the water. And I have lobbied my employer for shower facilities without success anyway.

My clothes get crumpled and very few outfits are not a disgrace as I step through the door. I've tried carrying clean clothes in my rucksack and changing into them at work, but with little luck. The rucksack creases most items badly. The only way round it seems to be to have a ready pressed supply of outfits hidden somewhere in my classroom, but there really isn't the space. And using my car to transport clothes to work is really self-defeating, isn't it? I'd have to re-stock items regularly, making the whole process a non-starter.

Added to that, changing into a completely new outfit in a cramped toilet cubicle is really quite unpleasant!

So for now I'll have to remain wrinkled until I can think of a solution. Any ideas you may have will be gratefully received.

And to complete my look as the scruffiest teacher in the school there is the awful state of my hair. I have discovered that a hot and sweaty head is a most unfortunate combination with my flattened "helmet-hair". I've tried both curling tongs and straighteners but the results have been less than impressive. Of course, I don't want to use more power in any event.

Any suggestions, dear friends?

That's all for today. Wishing you all a great week,

Love Amy xxx

Dear Amy and friends,

Thank you for inviting me to join your forum. I'm very happy to be asked especially as we're all rather isolated in this terrible lockdown. But I'm so slow with my laptop – my husband would have laughed to see me with it as I'm hopeless with technology! However, I'm determined to persevere and "get up to speed", as you young ones would say. I just hope that I will have something of interest to write here – are you sure that you want to hear from an old stick like me? Well, here goes…

I dared to venture out of my little house this morning and immediately I congratulated myself for only sighing and not tutting!

But it probably wouldn't have mattered if I had tufted. The young lad from next-door was so engrossed in his mobile phone that he was seemingly oblivious to everything else, including me.

I had to step off the pavement to walk around the boy who stood right in the middle, taking up all the space with his battered rucksack by his feet. He was texting furiously using just his thumbs. There was an intense look of concentration on his face-well, what I could see of his face.

He is actually quite nice-looking, with clear green eyes and a smattering of freckles across his straight nose and rosy cheeks. But the whole fresh-faced look was, as usual, spoiled by the untidy shock of black hair which flopped forward right over one eye. I don't know how he could see well enough to text, and what did the youngster even find to text about?

I don't see him often, but when we do cross paths, the lad is rarely seen without his headphones on and his mobile apparently super-glued into his hand.

I'm just wondering how old he is now. About 13, I think, as my dear Nathaniel was still with me when the young couple moved in next-door with their new baby.

How time flies!

I just took a quick stroll and popped into the local corner shop, seeing no-one else except for the shopkeeper. Returning home I passed an elderly gent who was carrying a newspaper. We scooted carefully around each other but didn't speak – I know we don't have to wear our masks outside but I prefer it – I never thought that I would ever say that! My mask does make conversations more difficult because I feel very muffled and can't seem to get my words out properly. Not that I've had much chance to speak to anyone anyway.

Back home I busied myself with the kettle and putting away my basket of groceries. I couldn't help smiling as I remembered being woken that first night by the new-born's crying.

"Don't be such an old crab apple!" my husband had laughed when I moaned to him about my interrupted sleep. "We'll get used to the noise and it's lovely to have youngsters cheering up our little lane."

Of course, Nathaniel had been right. Together we'd looked forward to seeing our new little neighbour grow and develop. We'd even thought that we might be able to help out with baby-sitting occasionally. We could have become good friends with the young parents and an extra aunty and uncle to their son.

But sadly it never happened. Poor Nathaniel was taken so ill and I suddenly found myself alone for the first time in almost 50 years. Somehow I couldn't face making those new relationships after all. So I sort-of retreated into myself and remained only on the vaguest friendly terms of nodding "Hello" or muttering an awkward "Good afternoon" on the few occasions when I did see my neighbours out and about.

How different it might all have been with my dear husband still by my side. But then I gave myself a mental shake. It's no good wallowing and feeling sorry for myself when so many people have suffered much worse. I really hope that I haven't become an old crab apple after all!

That's all for now! Sorry if I've bored you all! Wishing you well,

Lois Lennox

Greetings everybody,

Hope things are well with you all. I've enjoyed reading all the posts on this forum – so thanks again, Amy, for setting it up.

My children's home-schooling project this week has been on the universe – yes, really! They had to find out the order of the planets and find a fact about each one. I don't remember any of this from when we were at school – do you? Anyhow, it really was most interesting although I think that my enthusiasm far exceeded that of my twins!

Our positive today was seeing a beautiful blue tit on the bird feeder which our neighbours have in their little tree – and I'll add their garden itself to our plus list. Even though we can't go outside, at least our living room window looks over their garden – lovely.

I've invited my aunt to join this forum – hope that's ok with you all. She's on her own and struggling a bit with lockdown. I thought that she'd enjoy reading our news and I'm really hoping that it will give her a bit of an incentive to pop outside so she's got something to tell us about. She lives quite close to a lovely park but I know that she's rather afraid to go there just now. Her name is Esther and she's really fun

– in normal times – so let's hope that our little forum can inspire her.

Love to you all, Raquel x

Hello again everyone,

Today I had another exciting appointment, not a viewing but a valuation. So it was with a happy heart that I rang the doorbell of the property at 2 o'clock precisely.

The house was small but in good order. I walked round with the owner, who practically fizzed with impatience. He demanded a figure as I hovered in the hallway fastening my coat buttons.

Cheerfully, I told him that he had a lovely home and, taking account of the house's size, two bedrooms, good condition and great location, I'd recommend an asking price of £265,000 with a view to accepting reasonable offers in the region of £250,000 or perhaps even £255,000 (of course, I'm only naming the exact numbers as this property's address and its owner are totally absent from this forum).

But my hopes of impressing this potential client were instantly dashed. Angrily he cried that he wouldn't be giving the house away and expected £320,000 at the very least!

I tried to tell him that my valuation was based on comparable houses on the market, but he interrupted me at once. Most rudely he declared that his property was much better than any others on our books, although how could he possibly know that?

He told me to think of the integrated hob and oven in his kitchen and I could have told him that many houses on our listing have integrated appliances, but I refrained. Instead I said that homes in the £320,000 price bracket tended to have 3 bedrooms, a bigger garden and off-street parking.

I tried to convince him that we have lots of potential purchasers registered with our Agency who are looking for a house just like his and I felt very confident that we could soon find him a buyer.

Yet again this did not please this pompous man. He declared that the fortunate buyer of his property could easily get three bedrooms by converting the dining room into the third one and the front garden could be turned into parking for two cars. According to him, it would be a doddle to get the council to drop the kerb for the new driveway.

I might have pointed out that the house and green outside space would be even smaller with these plans and that it wasn't always easy to get the kerb sorted. But I didn't. I've been an estate agent for 17 years and experience has shown me that I wouldn't be able to convince him. No, he'd insist on the much higher asking price and then of course it would be our fault when his house failed to sell!

So, I forced a smile onto my face and took my leave, after sweetly suggesting that he give the matter some more thought.

And as I stepped out of his house he said that he would see what Parnells have to say later. His parting shot was that it's easy to sell properties as most homes practically sell themselves!

Poor Parnells are welcome to him.

I hope very much that you are all well and not bored rigid by my day!

Love to everyone, Justine x

Hello – how are you all? Hope that you are surviving despite these strange days of lockdown.

I've found a new problem with my bike which has only arisen since my local council suspended roadside collections of our recycling during the present lockdown. Are your councils still collecting recyclables, ladies?

Well, perhaps it's obvious but the paper, card, tins, plastics and glass all added together soon get very heavy. I really struggled with my bulging rucksack on the way to the recycling bins in the town car park. Returning home was a breeze, of course!

Thank goodness that Andy has set up the compost bin in our garden, so at least we don't have to worry about raw food and garden waste too – even if the children are complaining that it smells terrible in our garden now. Perhaps Andy can make some adjustments and conquer the pong – fingers crossed!

My mum kindly offered to take the glass, etcetera, in her car – but I valiantly turned her down. The whole point of recycling is to help save the environment, not use more fuel in getting our waste into the correct facilities. Mum said that she could combine taking the recycling when she went on her scheduled shopping trips, but I'd backed myself into a corner and didn't feel able to accept. So I'll have to soldier on for now – sigh!

Keep happy and safe,

Lots of love Amy xxx

PS Thanks for the tip for my cycle-hair problem, Lois. I tried it but the results weren't impressive – I still looked as if I'd been dragged through a hedge backwards! And when my head teacher saw me in the heated curlers, he laughed so hard that he cried. So, I won't be trying them again – thanks all the same!

A xxx

Dear Amy and friends,

Thanks for all your kind messages welcoming me to your forum. I feel very honoured to be part of your supportive and friendly group.

Before we went into lockdown, I always did what Nathaniel had called a "big shop" on the first Tuesday of every month when the supermarket was not quite so busy. Luckily, my last regular big shop was in the week before we entered the restrictions so I stocked up on my usual heavier things such as food tins, frozen items and washing powder. As I always took a taxi home afterwards, I tried to think ahead and so avoid carrying too much when I walked home from the local corner shop a couple of times in the weeks after my big shop. Even though it's only three streets away, I still struggle home sometimes.

I don't feel safe in the taxi or big supermarket any more, but I think I can manage. I'll just need to keep supplied with fresh fruit and vegetables, bread and milk from our local shop. What a pity that there is no longer a milk delivery service in this area.

The nice weather has meant that I've spent a lot of time in my little garden this week. I've been deadheading my spring bulbs and wondering about my summer borders as I won't be able to get my bedding plants from the garden centre as usual. Perhaps I don't need to worry so much about the larger, busier places, but I just can't help it.

I love working in the garden and it usually relaxes me. But this week the old memories of the child next door filled my mind as I snipped. What a nuisance he had been with his football! Many times had the ball found its way into our garden and yes, it had often landed among my precious flowers.

I took to dropping the ball back over the fence as soon as possible, so avoiding direct contact with the boy. Sometimes he called out a cheery "Thank you", but somehow I couldn't bring myself to reply. I'm sorry to admit that I felt too awkward to respond. Dear Nathaniel would have known what to say.

I can't recall when the football ceased to be an issue. Nowadays it is loud music throbbing through the wall between our two houses, but this doesn't bother me nearly so much – there is indeed an upside to getting a bit hard of hearing!

That's all for now! Wishing you all well,

Lois Lennox

Greetings everybody,

I don't have much news, so sorry for just a short post from me today.

I've had a right battle with the twins over getting dressed, of all things! They'd far rather stay in their pyjamas, both telling me that there's no point in putting "normal" clothes on when we're not going outside anyway. But I feel that it doesn't inspire them to try their best on their schoolwork or even to get out of bed at a reasonable time. (But they can get up at the crack of dawn when I want a lie-in!) Eventually, I had to compromise and agree to pyjama days at the weekends if they want. However, I'm not joining them in this!

The twins' home-schooling project was a musical one, which was very interesting. They had to compose, play and record a weather soundscape – do you do these with the children at your school, Amy? I'd certainly never heard of them before. They could play actual instruments if they have them (which we don't) or make their own. So, they used old jam and coffee jars with various amounts of water in, which made effective notes when struck with a pen – rather like a xylophone. Plus they made "maracas" with dried pasta and rice in plastic bottles and used my side tables as drums.

Daisy composed a wind soundscape and Arthur went with rain. They worked individually and then put their pieces together to make a storm soundscape. I was so proud of them and that's definitely my positive for today – so nice when they work together rather than fighting, for a change!

Love to you all, Raquel

Hello dear ladies,

Many thanks for all your kind messages of welcome. I'm thrilled to be invited onto this forum (I hope that I will have something to add each week without putting you to shame, Raquel). So here it is: my first ever post on an online forum.

Now that the authorities have relaxed our lockdown rules a bit and declared it safe for us to meet other people outside, I was determined to stroll around my local park today. First I looked out of my door and only stepped outside when I was certain that there was no-one else about. As I scurried up the street and into the park, I chided myself for such caution. After all, they said it is safe now, didn't they?

But I felt so nervous. I know exactly how you feel, Lois. Are you younger girls as anxious as me?

I had to force myself to breathe slowly and deeply, then started walking through the municipal grounds at a more leisurely pace. Yet still I felt uneasy. A jogger headed in my direction and I'm a bit embarrassed to admit that I turned my back completely to avoid him. This almost-encounter left me feeling rather shaky all of a sudden so I sat down on the nearest available wooden bench to recover.

Despite my shakes, I congratulated myself for finally managing to get out of my flat at last after so many weeks inside. A bit unsteady, but at least I'd made it this far.

Silly really: I've travelled half-way around the world in the past. But that was before the Corona virus, when nobody had heard of "Covid 19" and "lockdown" was something they did in prisons. Now, a simple trip to the park feels like a major achievement. The world has certainly changed and in such a relatively short span of time.

A young woman was walking towards me, pushing a pram with a toddler holding onto the pram's handle. I tried hard to stay where I was, but I just couldn't do it. I gave the mother an apologetic half smile, then stood and turned away from the little family group. Was it really safe to be in the park at all?

When they had passed by me, I sank back onto the seat. Just a few short months ago, I would have said "Hello" and looked inside the pram and asked after the baby. I might even have asked the toddler's name and probably would have commented on the beautiful weather. But sadly all that feels quite alien now.

Suddenly I became aware that I'd been keeping my hands safely on my lap. Quite unconsciously I'd avoided actually touching the bench with my bare hands. What do you all think: does danger really lurk on every surface outside our own homes? And will people like me ever be less frightened?

Feeling totally unable to enjoy the sunshine and the tranquillity of nature around me, I rose from the bench and retraced my steps so that I could get home as soon as possible.

So today has been quite a special day for me, with my first foray outside after shielding for months and my first post on this forum. Onwards and upwards from here!

Thanks for reading,

Esther

Hello ladies,

Exciting news – I have decided to renovate our wardrobe. So much better for the planet if we re-fresh what we already have, rather than cut down more trees. I'm sure you agree!

I wanted to devote the weekend to this project, so I've worked late every evening this week to get all my planning and marking done. Via the superstore I struggled home on Friday with a tin of paint in my rucksack. It's a beautiful soft cream – but honestly, I never realised before how heavy paint is!

Andy wasn't at all interested in helping – he hates all DIY – so I determined that I could do it all myself. I cleaned the wardrobe thoroughly then sanded down the wood. This looks quite easy on all those makeover shows on TV, but the orangey varnish on the pine was very stubborn. I persevered despite my aching shoulders and fingers, but the results were not as good as I'd hoped. The paint will work wonders, I'm sure! But for now I'm exhausted, so I'll have to delay the painting until next weekend. Groan!

Keep up your posts on this forum. I'm sure that we all enjoy getting each other's news.

Have a wonderful week,

Lots of love, Amy xxx

Greetings everyone,

Thanks for your kind comments welcoming my aunt Esther to our forum. I know that she's keen to be a member of our little group.

As we're shielding, all our shopping is done on-line and delivered right to our door. Sounds great, but the whole process of ordering actually takes longer than it would do to drive to the supermarket, do all the shopping, drive home again, unpack and have a cup of tea!

The twins wanted to try vegetable "spaghetti" as one of their pop idols was raving about it. So, I ordered four large courgettes to make "courgetti spaghetti" – but they gave us four big cucumbers instead! Any recipe ideas to use up loads of cucumber we didn't want?

Daisy and Arthur's home-schooling project this week was an art / maths one which they really enjoyed. They had to use whatever they could find around the flat – paper, cardboard boxes, wool, buttons etc. – and make a tall building. It could be a model of a real building or one of their own design. Then they could paint it if they wanted and they had to measure it and photograph it for their report. Daisy made an Eiffel Tower, mostly out of rolled up newspapers which I thought was rather clever of her. Arthur made a pyramid out of various boxes and added papier maché to make the sides smooth (turned out to be rather lucky that our roadside recycling collection service is suspended in lockdown, so we had lots of materials for their models).

The final element of the project was to measure the models and we even went on to compare them with the actual buildings. I surprised myself with this last bit and being able to help my kids with their maths. It's surprising what you can remember from your own schooldays, sometimes!

That was going to be my positive thing for today, but then I found something better when the kids spotted a fox in our neighbours' garden. It was quite confidently trotting round, so maybe it often goes there. We'll certainly look out for it again, but have some lovely photos of it too.

That's it for now.

Love to you all, Raquel x

Hello again everybody,

Today's viewers were a young couple recently married and looking for their first home. Cheerily, I welcomed them to the property and said that they would have seen on our listings that this was a bijou one-bedroom house, just ideal for a young couple like themselves.

Their reply was to inform me that they were planning to get a puppy, a cute spaniel they were going to call "Madge". As the young man showed me a photo of her on his mobile, his wife asked whether the house had a garden. You get used to meeting all kinds of people in this job!

I said yes, explaining that the garden was indeed big enough for a dog but not so big to be too much work.

The young woman was just saying how perfect it sounded, but her words and my smile fell away as the front door swung open.

Before us lay the hallway, looking as though a tornado had hit it. Several coats were slung untidily over the bannister rail but others were gathered in a messy heap on the floor where they had fallen off or perhaps had been thrown at the bannister and missed. An assortment of shoes, boots and trainers were scattered randomly everywhere, necessitating a very cautious route as we picked our way through to the kitchen. I scooped up a skateboard but couldn't see anywhere safe to put it.

I think that all three of us gasped when we entered the kitchen. The sink was overflowing with dirty plates and cutlery. Used mugs were alongside the kettle, some containing the coagulating remains of ancient drinks and some sporting mould. Even worse were the filthy saucepans on the hob, which I didn't dare to examine more closely. Worst of all was the bin which was overflowing and surrounded by rubbish which smelled terrible (maybe comparable to your compost bin, Amy).

I wasn't at all surprised that they stopped the viewing right there as they had seen enough and the place clearly wasn't for them after all.

I tried to counter that it would clean up well, but my heart wasn't really in it. The young man took his pretty wife's hand and we all began to pick our way back through the obstacle course in the hallway.

This nice couple turned back to say goodbye as they left. I waved with my free hand, feeling distinctly foolish as I stood there in the worst hallway I had seen for a long time, still clutching the skateboard with my other hand!

Well, that's it for today,

Love to you all, Justine x

Hello ladies. How are you all?

After all that effort last weekend, this weekend brought a mixed bag of results. Yes, I did squeeze three coats of paint in with playing cricket with my children in our back garden – all of us avoiding the pong of the compost heap (It's a bit better, but not much!). Both kids complained that they'd rather have been playing on their mobiles or texting their friends, but I enjoyed the cricket even if they weren't so keen. The fresh air in most of the garden made a welcome break from paint fumes!

I also managed to do all my school prep and enjoy a glass of wine on the patio with mum and Andy (another empty bottle for recycling!). I even had a long soak in the bath for almost ten minutes before someone hammered on the door demanding instant access to the bathroom.

And what of the wardrobe? What a disappointment! The tasteful cream paint barely covers the original pine despite three boring coats and an aching wrist. I must confess that it looks rather streaky and Andy has threatened to burn it and buy a new one after lockdown. Mum said that I hadn't made too bad a job for my first time, then spoiled it by adding that I'd probably do better on my next project. Oh well!

Have a fabulous week – enjoy the forecasted sunshine, if you can,

Love Amy xxx

Hello again dear ladies,

This morning I felt incredibly sad just putting on the kettle. All because I realised that I don't have many tea bags left. Now that I don't have to shield any longer, the kind deliveries have stopped.

Very soon I'll have to venture into a shop for the first time in ages. So silly, I know, but I'm not at all sure that I'll be up to that.

Of course, shopping has an extra complication in these troubled times. I tried on my face mask and stared disconsolately at my own reflection. I suppose that most of you are now used to your masks, but I've been shielding so haven't needed mine yet. My mask feels so strange. It seems such a momentous step to actually wear it, if I ever find myself able to go into a shop.

Suddenly, I had a flashback to my childhood and recalled visiting my granny when I was very young, perhaps about six years old. Playing in an upstairs room, I'd opened a drawer and found an old gas mask from the war. My gran told me that everyone had had to carry their gas masks everywhere and that as an infant, I had even been issued a Mickey Mouse-shaped face mask designed for babies. I couldn't help smiling as I remembered how disappointed I'd been when my old mask had failed to be found.

Of course, the wartime threat of a gas attack was totally different from this virus, but the potential life-threatening consequences are just as serious. So masks are not a new idea and that left me feeling just a little comforted, somehow.

But that didn't last long. The television news today was as gloomy as ever. The discussions of "spikes", "Covid hotspots" and "new variants" are so worrying. I don't know what my beloved husband, Bert, would have made of it all. What do you ladies think? Will all the restrictions be back in place before the planned total removal of the national lockdown even comes into effect? I really can't bear the thought of having to isolate again.

Thanks for reading,
Esther

Dear Amy and friends,

Several weeks into lockdown and I'm now adapting to my new normal – I hope that you are too.

However, I've begun to run out of things. The freezer is almost empty and my stock of food tins is running very low. I've made do with some odd combinations of ingredients recently – it must have been a bit like this in war times!

But two truly amazing things have happened this week. The community spirit of my little town has been such a super surprise.

First of all, the lovely ladies from the local primary school started coming with a hot meal for me every day. It's all done very safely. They ring my doorbell and are usually gone by the time I get my door open to collect the welcome food. These anonymous women are so kind and are a real lifeline.

And the other amazing surprise was that a wonderful volunteer rang me via my doctor. This kind, young man organised the collection and delivery of my prescription. Even better yet, he will organise my repeat prescription if we're still in lockdown when the next one is due. This is such a bonus and I genuinely don't know how I'd manage without him.

Perhaps you lovely, young ladies don't feel so much fear as me, but my corner shop is absolutely the limit of my bravery just now. These kind strangers providing me with marvellous meals and my medicine have made it possible to survive with all the restrictions and made me feel less isolated too. My faith in human nature is totally restored – strange that it took the consequences of this awful virus.

That's it from me for this week. Hope you are all well,

Best wishes,

Lois L.

Newsflash – we are getting a new bathroom now that the restrictions are easing a bit!

Andy and I have chosen a swish new walk-in shower and there's just going to be enough space for a separate bath. Mum thinks that the toilet and basin will be rather cramped, but Andy is determined to get his shower. The children wanted to have two basins, but what would be the point of losing the shower just to enable them to brush their teeth at the same time? That's really the only time they might be in the bathroom together and they're growing up so fast that they'll soon be demanding their privacy anyhow.

All these issues made the whole shopping experience rather fraught, but I'm looking forward to getting the work done nevertheless!

Don't forget to post your news – I'm sure that it really does brighten all our days!

Stay safe and smiling,

Lots of Jove, Amy xxx

Greetings to you all,

All going OK here – but all three of us are feeling rather bored! The twins had a poem to write for their home-schooling project this week – don't laugh, but I've had a go too! I'm not sure if it's suitable for this forum, but here it is:

Corona

1

Death stalks our silent streets
Slinks along on silent feet
Its icy touch meets no resistance
Despite new rules of social distance

2

Death stalks our quiet streets
Creeping close on quiet feet
Poisoned tendrils slither still
Waiting for their chance to kill

3

Death stalks our noiseless streets
Nobbling us on noiseless feet
Lurk frozen fingers to clutch our health
Victims destroyed by skulking stealth

4

Death stalks our soundless streets
Skitters past on soundless feet
We cower in self-isolation
Yet oozes still our desolation

5

Death stalks our empty streets
Edging near on fearless feet
Seeps through the cracks of society
Trailing terror and anxiety

6

Death stalks our vacant streets
Voiding us on fearsome feet
Helpless we fall in the yawning tomb
Tumbling to everlasting doom

Please don't be too critical of my meagre offering!
Love to you all, Raquel x

Hello once again dear ladies,

Today dawned fine and bright and I was determined to walk right around the park grounds. 'No losing your bottle!' I told myself firmly and smiled at my silly self.

I opened my front door and forced myself to step onto the pavement even though the postman was coming. But I was glad that I did so, for he wished me a cheerful "Good morning." As he went whistling down the street, I promised myself that I would say "Hello" to him tomorrow.

I walked into the municipal grounds and noticed with pleasure that everything felt slightly easier today. I was able to stroll without shaking at all.

A jogger headed towards me and I was determined to stay on the path with him. He nodded at me but he was gone before I'd smiled in response. Still, I hadn't turned away so that was definite progress, wasn't it?

Feeling just a little flustered, I sat on the nearest bench and deliberately laid my hands on the wooden slats. The wood was pleasantly warm in the sun and I could feel where a knot had been sanded down. Relaxing a little, I watched a squirrel darting across the grass and decided that I would buy him some nuts – if I found myself able to go shopping later. I had my new face mask in my coat pocket, ready to wear if I did venture into a shop, but I still felt quite unsure that I would actually manage it.

As I enjoyed the gentle breeze on my face, I suddenly remembered a trip to London with my mother many years ago. I'd had to have some specialist tests on my ears at a children's hospital in the capital so the pair of us travelled there by train. I don't remember much about the tests themselves, but I smiled as I recalled what happened afterwards.

"Let's visit the shops and see the Christmas lights," my mother had said.

And it had been magical. The shops were all decorated for the season with coloured lights and I remember the fantastic displays in the windows of the larger stores. One had a polar bear model in a snowy scene with Santa's elves and piles of presents. Another had eight decorated reindeers harnessed up to a life-sized sleigh with Father Christmas loading his sack of gaily-wrapped gifts.

My mother also took me to Trafalgar Square and we both marvelled at the size and beauty of the Christmas tree there. We shared a bag of hot, roasted chestnuts and the afternoon was truly wonderful.

However, as I tried to recall which year that had happened, I had a clear memory of the awful stink in the city. The air had been filled with noxious, yellow fumes which my mother called "smog". It was awful and I recall the policemen wearing leather masks to protect themselves as they stood in the streets, directing the limited traffic with whistles and torches as visibility was so bad. My mother and I didn't have masks but, like many others around us, we wrapped our scarves tightly over our mouths and noses.

"I can't see my feet, Mum!" I exclaimed on one particularly hazy street.

We laughed at first, but were mightily relieved to get on one of the few buses which were running with conductors walking ahead with torches to direct the poor drivers. It wasn't at all funny really.

Arriving at the train station, there had been a break in the clouds and we had so appreciated the little patch of sunlight. But as we waited on the platform, the smog began to seep back into the atmosphere and swirl around us. It was the first time in my life that I recall being truly frightened.

Thinking back, I realise that the spread of the Corona virus was very like that creeping smog as it swept across the world into mainland Europe and then into Great Britain. Do you agree that there seemed to be a terrible inevitability about the virus despite so many precautions? But the foul smog had led to the Clean Air Act which conquered it. I think that the vaccines are definitely progress although I really hope that the scientists will soon develop a cure for Covid 19.

Back in the past, my mother and I were so lucky to get a train home when so many others had been cancelled. But still the smog had hampered our breathing as it somehow seeped into our train carriage despite the closed windows and doors. I remember that birds had crashed into buildings and cattle had died in the smothering fumes in their fields. We arrived home looking like coal miners with greasy, black ooze over us and our clothes. It was such hard work to clean it off too.

On my wooden bench today, I was just musing that I must have been about 12, so the smog must have been in the December of 1952. Yes, that seems right.

And that dreadful time had eventually come to an end, ladies. Somehow, the world's problems with the Corona pandemic will start to recede as well, with vigilance and us all pulling together.

Thanks for reading,

Esther

Hello ladies,

It's been a rather hellish week but it's ended marvellously! We've had the plumber here most days, fitting our new bathroom. Despite the hell of no water, dust and tools everywhere (honestly, almost every room in the house was in chaos for most of the week so we've had to tiptoe round boxes and pipes and all sorts, even in our bedrooms!) it's wonderful now that it's finished.

The suite and most of the pipes etcetera are white – had to be white! We chose fancy new taps – 'silver' mixer taps and an enormous square shower-head which was, of course, my dear husband's preference. We've jazzed the room up with turquoise mosaic tiles and soft, sea green wooden flooring. So stylish even if I do say so myself!

Andy and the children have been in their elements with the new power shower. Mum and I have both enjoyed wonderful soaks in the bath. (We love the shower too – but don't tell Andy!)

And the old bathroom suite is now looking rather forlorn in our back garden, but I have a plan for that – more next week.

Keep safe and happy,

Love Amy xxx

PS the compost bin is now almost pong-free – when its lid is on, that is!

A xxx

Hello again everybody,

Today I had no appointments at all, so I spent the day catching up on some paperwork at home (along with a good chunk of TV). I feel guilty saying this as so many people have to work from home in lockdown, but it feels like a luxury when you normally have to commute to an office, etc. (Sorry Raquel – I'm sure that the 'luxury' vanished for you long ago).

I treated myself to a long walk this afternoon and passed a few other people enjoying the sunshine too. We're out of lockdown here, as you know, and our government has really left it up to us to decide if we want to wear face masks. I usually do in the supermarket and bank, but some of the people out walking today had masks on. Do you have to wear them when you are strolling through a park where you are? Fear of this virus is terrible, isn't it?

Returning home (it's an elegant house in the ever-popular mock Georgian style – I can't help it: I'm an estate agent!) I called out a greeting to my family but only my husband replied.

He directed me to the snug and told me not to go into the kitchen. Poor Ben had ventured there when he got back from work and found James going rather frantic. Apparently, our darling son was in the most delicate stage of preparing a new recipe and it would all be my husband's fault if the soufflé sank!

I flopped onto the sofa beside Ben and dared to enquire what was on our menu. You'll never guess – James was preparing a seaweed soufflé with roasted kohlrabi flakes served on a bed of artichoke mash and a red wine reduction! Honestly, how could you keep a straight face for that?

I must say that James' catering course is going very well and he has great hopes of opening his own restaurant and gaining a Michelin star.

But the menu wasn't the only reason that Ben was smiling. He told me that our son has decided that "James Smith" simply won't cut it in the gourmet world of fine dining. He's still toying with ideas, so don't worry too much just yet, but his first thought was "Jimmy Sparkle". As if the food wasn't torture enough!

Ben poured us both a large gin and tonic, with the comforting words that the sun was sure to be over the yard arm somewhere in the world. Only yesterday we'd agreed not to indulge ourselves with any more mid-week alcohol, but we caved in at the first hurdle.

Two drinks later, we made our way into the dining room when James announced that our meal was ready. Actually, it wasn't as bad as it sounded, and was miles better than yesterday's offering.

As our son returned to the kitchen for the dessert, Ben remarked that a couple of gins certainly made James' food taste better, so he should make gin compulsory for all customers in his future restaurant.

The sweet turned out to be caramel creme brulée, which I genuinely thought sounded nice. Unfortunately, James had obviously been so attentive to his soufflé that he had neglected his dessert. My husband put a spoonful into his mouth and nearly broke a tooth on the caramel which was harder than granite. We told James that we would wash up, so were able to sneak our un-eaten desserts into the bin without hurting our son's feelings.

My wish for tomorrow was for a supper of beans on toast followed by a piece of fruit – but we may not get that lucky.

Have a fantastic evening everyone,

Love Justine x

Hello dear ladies,

The upcycling has begun! So far, I've had the old bathroom basin moved into the hallway, right by the front door. It still stands on its pedestal and I thought it would be fun to keep the taps too! I spent ages lining the bowl with cushioned white vinyl (much harder than it looks on the TV!) because it's now our key store. Quite unique!

Andy says it's a monstrosity but I'm not disheartened! The bath project is set for next weekend – wish me luck!

Have a wonderful week,

Lots of love, Amy xxx

Greetings to you all,

Thanks very much everyone for your positive comments about my poem. Needless to say, my twins weren't so impressed! Honestly, it's been years since I've written anything like it – not since I was at school – and I amazed myself by really enjoying it. So here is this week's work:

Going Viral

Pestilence prowls our deserted streets
Dishing out death to all he meets
Greedily grasping our humanity
Putrid plague of vile calamity
Coughing, spluttering, we gasp for air
Pestilence truly doesn't care
Pain scything our skulls in two
Desperate doctors nothing can do
Terror tumbles in a deadly spiral
Pestilence globally going viral

I'll try to provide you with some news again next time!
Love to you all, Raquel x

Dear Amy and friends,

Hope you are all well even in these odd times!

Just a short message from me this week – it's hard when our worlds have shrunk so much and most of us are doing so little. I'm not clever enough to write any poems but I very much enjoyed reading Raquel's clever creative works.

A third instalment of our community's wonderful spirit arrived yesterday. A fantastic box of supplies was left on my doorstep from the kind volunteers at St Andrew's church. The box was full of goodies and I'm so grateful. They gave me some teabags, a jar of coffee, a bar of luxury soap and a pack of toilet rolls, along with a selection of fresh foods and even some shortbread. There was also a little note explaining that I would get another box of 'stock and treat items' in a fortnight and they plan to continue with two-weekly deliveries until we are out of lockdown. I am almost bowled over by the amazing kindness of strangers.

Hoping that this week has been equally kind to you all,

Lois x

Hello folks,

Justine is in bed with flu and is going to be out of action for a few days at least, if not the whole week. So how about an instalment from me for a change?!

My week was a disaster to start with, but it finished well. My first appointment was on Monday and my brief was to share my thoughts on making the most of a tiny garden. As usual on a first meeting with new clients, I took along my samples of different paving options, and my book of containers and hanging baskets. I had my photographs of the pond I'd created in a barrel last year. I was ready, or so I thought, but the house turned out to be a mansion. Then my potential client showed me into his "tiny" back garden. Just over two acres, it was!

I must have looked flabbergasted, as he informed me that the garden used to be nearly ten acres but he'd recently sold off a huge chunk to a developer. So I fudged it a bit and showed the old man my portfolio to get some idea of the style of planting he'd like, took some soil samples and made some notes. To complete my sense of wasting my time, the man confided that he would have to run every idea past his wife when she got back from golf.

My second appointment of the week went ok, but I'm getting to the stage where I might have to charge more for yet another Oriental garden. These potential clients wanted a red, Japanese tea house with bamboos, acers and cherry trees. Also, they had set their hearts on a contemplative water feature, plus a dry riverbed of raked gravel and a couple of stone dragons.

They didn't mention a rock shaped like Mount Fuji but I might give them that if I get the contract. I'll inform them that they can paint the top white to resemble snow or leave it to the birds to decorate it for them.

My final call of the week was to a young couple who really do have a small garden. You'll be amazed to hear what they wanted me to do for them – a rock garden! Stay in business long enough and everything comes back into fashion eventually.

Honestly, I haven't put in a rock garden for years. But this couple wanted an old-fashioned rock garden full of alpines, no less. And it was only last month that I took one out from their neighbours' garden and built a deck in its place. Will it be pink and yellow chequerboard patios next?

I'm really looking forward to the next couple of days and a good old cottage-style garden. No construction, no decorative features, just real gardening.

That's it for this week so I'll sign off now. Hopefully, Justine will be back on her feet soon and will be able to resume her writing on this forum. Thanks for reading and have a good week,

Best wishes, Ben

Hello yet again dear ladies,

I saw the young family from the other day in the park again today. I wonder how the woman managed with a young baby and a toddler during lockdown. It must have been extremely difficult.

As they neared me, the toddler stumbled and let go of the pram's handle. Without any hesitation, I dashed forward and caught him in my arms.

"My name is Alec," the youngster declared confidently, beaming delightedly at me.

The young mother thanked me and told Alec to say "thank you" too. He did so, then took his mother's outstretched hand and they continued on their way. I couldn't help smiling at the contented scene they made together.

That's the first actual contact I've had for months, and it felt so good, ladies.

But suddenly I wondered what the regulations are now. That contact had breached the 'social distancing' rules – or did they not apply with young children? I really have no idea; everything is so complicated nowadays. I had to really steel myself to resist the urge to spray my hands with the cleansing gel from the little bottle in my pocket. So silly, I know. I couldn't help shrugging and shaking my head wryly.

Another woman approached unseen from the opposite direction. She sat down on the other end of my bench, chuckling merrily.

"Talking to yourself!" she exclaimed. "Don't worry, I don't think it's a bad thing – it's actually a sign of intelligence in these strange times!"

I could feel my cheeks flushing, but the woman was so friendly that I soon shook off my embarrassment.

"Look at us," the lady said. "We'll be following the social-distancing rules if we stay like this, both keeping to our own ends of the bench like beautiful, human bookends!"

I couldn't help laughing as well. It's been a long time since anyone has called me 'beautiful' even if the comment had been made in jest.

The newcomer introduced herself as Carol, saying, "We won't shake hands!" and we both giggled.

It was lovely to laugh together and it really made my day, ladies.

Thanks for reading,

Esther

Hello friends,

The upcycling saga continues! With Andy's reluctant help, the old bath is now at the bottom of the garden in front of the stone bench. And I've turned it into – can you guess? – yes, it's now a stylish coffee table!

How did I transform it? First, I ordered a large sheet of blue Perspex online and it arrived on Wednesday – without doubt, it's the biggest thing that I've ever had in the post!

I worried about buying lots of tools – would that be ecological? – but a fellow teacher at my school loaned me a few necessary items, so my green credentials remain intact. It was a terrible struggle, but I finally managed to cut the Perspex into the right size and shape to fit right over the bath. Honestly, I attached it with these special sticky pads (another online purchase – is buying online eco-friendly, do you think?) and it makes the most striking table top. I even succeeded in using my kind colleague's router to create a safe rounded edge on the Perspex.

I think it looks great but the children think it's awful – "hideous" is the word Julie used! Andy says that it might leak a bit around the taps, but we've still got the plughole so it won't matter even if it does leak. Triumph!

Wishing you all a great week, Amy xxx

Dear Amy and friends,

As I've mentioned before, I thank my lucky stars that I'm fortunate enough to have a garden. I feel very sorry for everyone who has to stay at home without any outdoor space to enjoy safely.

But lately we've had day after day of rain here and I've been quite unable to get out into my garden for what seems like ages. After a whole week inside I have to confess that my spirits were really sagging.

But then my doorbell rang this morning. I was surprised as I had already received a tasty shepherd's pie and a sultana cookie for my lunch. I wasn't expecting anything else.

When I opened my door, I was astonished to see the young lad from next-door. He was standing well back and was getting rather wet. So often it seems that modern youngsters don't wear coats even when it's pouring with rain!

The boy smiled at me and pointed down to my feet. It was only then that I noticed the beautiful flowers peeping out of a carrier bag on my doorstep.

I thanked the lad and bent down to pick up the pretty posy. He didn't reply, just waved and set off back to his own house.

It wasn't until I was arranging the flowers in a vase that I found a little envelope. I was puzzled and opened the envelope to reveal a note:

I know you love flowers, so I hope these will cheer you up!
Best wishes from Nathan.
PS Mum hopes you like her home-made jam.

Well I just had to pause for thought. Of course I was delighted with the beautiful blooms but I was totally amazed to learn that the boy's name was so similar to my own dear husband's.

Perhaps it isn't too late to develop that friendly, elderly "aunty" relationship after all – what do you think, ladies?

Turning back to the carrier bag, you'll never guess what I found – there was a hexagonal glass jar with a square of red and white checked fabric, tied prettily on the top with red ribbon. I read the label, handwritten in red felt pen:

Sandra's crab apple jelly.

I laughed until I had tears rolling down my face. What an amazing gift and how my dear Nathaniel would have laughed too.

As I placed the vase on my windowsill, I noticed the rain still falling and I just couldn't help chuckling. Every cloud does indeed have a silver lining!

That's it for today. Have a really nice week and keep smiling,

Love from Lois x

Greetings to you all,

Thanks for your kind feedback about my second little poem. You'll be relieved to hear that I've not written another one – not yet…

Arthur, Daisy and I have made a real effort to go out for a quick walk every day now that the restrictions have been eased a little. Thank goodness that we don't have to shield any longer – I love our flat but it has turned into a cage at times recently… We've succeeded so far, despite the rain and I really love our walks. I think the twins do too, despite their protests about the weather. Honestly, the joy of being out in the fresh air is so wonderful that I really don't even mind the torrential rain we had today!

I told the kids that my nan always said that we're not made out of sugar and so we won't melt in the rain (of course, she meant 'dissolve' not 'melt' – a little science input there, but my children weren't really interested in science as we rushed inside to dry off!).

This week their home-schooling project has been on comparing the lengths of various British rivers – yikes! Geography is really not my forté. I can't wait till they go back to school!

Hope you're all managing to dodge the deluge!
Love to you all, Raquel x

Hi folks,

It's me, Ben, again! Justine is getting better but isn't back at work yet, so I'm filling in again for her on this forum – we hope that's OK with you all.

Sadly, business is so slow here as to be almost extinct, so I haven't any news to report. But I came across this article online and thought that you might enjoy it. Glee does have some good points, but there's a giggle or two here as well. I'm not sure how we stand with copyright, but I think we'll be alright if you don't print it out or send it to anyone else. (ok-ish!)

Best wishes, Ben

Garden with Glee

Glee Leonard continues her series on garden planning and planting for beginners.

You learned all about planning the overall layout of your garden last week, so by now you have dug your borders ready for planting. But before we can move on to the exciting processes of choosing your plants and how to place them to best effect in your flowerbeds, we need to consider your soil. Many novice gardeners ignore this step, but it really is absolutely vital if you want to achieve results that will make your neighbours green with envy.

First, take a good handful of earth from your borders and rub it carefully between your fingers. If it is crumbly and falls apart easily, then you have sandy soil. This tends to be acidic and there are many species which suit this type, but you will increase your chances of success with a greater range of plants by improving your soil. Simply add a good amount of compost with added lime and horse manure and fork it in well. For best results, I like to use compost-stickyloameii, which is readily available at all good nurseries and garden centres.

However, if your soil feels claggy and sticks to your fingers, you have clay soil which tends to be alkaline. Of course, many species will thrive in these conditions, but again you can increase your range of plants by adding some compost mixed with grit to improve drainage. My recommendation would be for compost with a high percentage of organic matter – horse manure or any muck really – and even some well-rotted bark chippings. Compost-grittyextrawhiffeii is a good choice, also sold in all the usual outlets. Don't be tempted to spread it too thinly; add a good layer over your borders and fork it in well.

On the other hand, it may be that your soil is neither too crumbly nor too sticky. This means that you are lucky enough to have the ideal soil for most plants, but you can still achieve better results by adding a soil improving compost to help your plants establish well. My choice would be for compost-perfectlysmugeii which you can find in all good garden centres and nurseries.

And so we are ready for the important step of selecting the plants themselves. So much depends on the size of your garden, of course. But a good guide is to choose plants which will grow to a variety of sizes so adding interest to your flowerbeds. I have set out some excellent plant combinations for the three basic soil types – please refer to the chart following this article for more information.

The next item of consideration is colour. Many blooms are available in a variety of colours, so you need to choose carefully to create the most pleasing effects. You could follow a monochrome design, where all your flowers are of the same colour with differences of shade bringing subtle interest. Or you could decide upon a complementary plan with two colours which harmonize together, such as pinks and purples. Yet another approach is to select plants of contrasting colours, perhaps oranges and blues. Many gardening gurus will advise you to look at the colour wheel to guide you, but this is not absolutely necessary. Perhaps the best way is simply to choose what you like most – beauty is in the eye of the beholder, after all.

Having established your colour and height preferences, there are three further important issues for you to consider: the foliage, the amount of sun/shade and the flowering season of your plant selections. Let us look at leaves first. They do not just grow in various shades of green: they come in different colours from almost blacks, through russet-reds to silvery-whites, so take them into account with your colour scheme. I direct you once again to my chart on the following pages for more details.

Experienced gardeners will also choose plants with a variety of leaf shapes, but this may be something for you to plan in future years as you gain horticultural confidence.

Next, we need to factor in the amount of sun which each border receives. Hopefully, you will have noted the direction of the sun in your garden throughout the day, as I advised last week. So you should study your notes and determine whether each border is in full or partial sun or shade for most of the day. Some plants simply will not thrive in too much direct sunshine whereas others will not grow well in too much shade. You are setting yourself up for failure if you ignore this vital issue, but my handy chart will help you in this area too.

Finally, try to pick plants with different flowering seasons. You want to avoid everything blossoming at the same time, leaving your borders barren for the rest of the year. Yet again, please refer to my chart for further guidance. Don't forget to include some evergreens too, for year-round interest.

Now then, having selected which plants you want for each of your flowerbeds, you need to understand the basic principles of planting up your borders. Naturally these also depend on the size of your plot, as larger gardens with many pathways will afford more viewpoints than smaller locations so can be more relaxed about the usual "rules". However, basic principles can be applied to most grounds and then you can experiment with alternative approaches in subsequent years.

One of the most important considerations is the height of your chosen plants when fully grown. You will achieve the most pleasing results by placing the tallest species at the back of your borders and the smallest plants at the front. This may sound obvious, but many new gardeners fail on this point. So a tall-growing shrub such as jollyenormious will thrive and look its best towards the back with smaller plants like the popular foliaveragies before it and sodaintyimums right at the front of your border.

Another aspect to plan carefully is how many plants of each species you should select. A frequent novice error is to choose just one of a great many species. This will result in quite a jumble even if you do locate your plants according to size. As a general rule, select just one or two of the largest plants for each border and place more of the smaller species as you work your way forward. I have had great success with planting in odd numbers, so choose three or five of the same variety of littler plants and group them together. Another pleasing arrangement is drift planting where there are great swathes of the same plants. Strangely, this can even give the illusion of more size to smaller plots of, say, half an acre or so.

By now you will have chosen the plants best suited to your soil type, taking account of maximum sizes, flower colours, foliage, amount of sun or shade and the flowering seasons of all your selections. At last you are ready to begin the thrilling stage of planting. A good tip is simply to place your plants just on top of your borders according to your plan, then stand back and survey the layout. You should gain a pretty good idea of whether your proposed layout works in reality. If it does not, you can make any necessary amendments without needing to dig up and re-position your precious plants.

Many species require a hole to be dug of the same depth as the pot you purchased them in, but there are a few notable exceptions. My chart will once again provide you with the guidance you need on this point.

Gently ease each plant out of its pot or seed tray, place it in the prepared hole and fill around it with your prepared soil and compost mixture. Firm the soil around the plant with your heel for larger species and with your hands with smaller ones. Remember that larger shrubs and small trees may need staking – my handy and extensive chart will instruct you on this issue.

Finally, as each border is complete, give it a thorough watering. The old saying of "puddle in" your plants remains a good guide. Do not be tempted to skimp on this point, or on subsequent days. Many novice gardeners neglect their watering and disaster will surely follow.

To those who are completely new to gardening, planning and planting up your borders can seem rather like juggling with so many factors to consider. But I would like to assure you that once you have mastered the basics, you will achieve successful results. And most importantly, you will grow to love horticulture.

However there is a very simple alternative if this "juggling" is too daunting: for a reasonable fee you could employ a professional to take care of all the worry and work for you. Take a look at my website for more details – you can find the address at the bottom of my comprehensive chart. Who knows, maybe you could soon be relaxing in your beautiful and stylish garden without having to lift even one green finger.

Next week: How to build and age your own tumbledown garden folly.

Forthcoming issues: Your summerhouse – gazebo or grand pavilion?

Vegetables – self-sufficiency in under an acre.

Hello once more dear ladies,

I've some good news for you today. From that unlikely beginning, a new friendship has blossomed. Carol and I have met up again and are now meeting in the park on most mornings. Sometimes Carol brings a flask of coffee to share, careful to pour my cup while wearing rubber gloves and putting the drinks at a social distance between us. On other days, I bring a bag of nuts for us to throw to the squirrels, equally careful to put them in the middle of our bench. We use wet wipes and hand sanitizers, not feeling remotely uncomfortable with all the "new normal" ways of doing things.

We chat away quite naturally together. We've discovered that we have travelled to some of the same places in far-off lands, but other aspects of our lives are very different. I'm a widow whereas Carol is divorced. Carol has a son who emigrated to Canada, whilst I have no children of my own. But it doesn't matter: Carol has a wonderful sense of humour and is great fun. In what seems like no time at all, I'm joyfully anticipating our meetings and it's marvellous to feel so positive once more.

Thanks for reading,

Esther

Hello friends,

What a busy week! We've had Sports Day at my school – the oddest one we've ever had! The few children still attending (offspring of key workers, etc.) took part in a range of events on our school field. The head teacher filmed them all and posted it online for the rest of our children who are learning at home. We teachers carefully recorded all their scores, times, distances and so on, and these were uploaded online too. Then the home-school kids could take part in the events in their living rooms or gardens, if they're lucky enough to have a garden. They recorded their results and we added them to our records, eventually determining the winners of each event.

It was a massive amount of work! And some of the scores were really bizarre. My reduced class of children suspect that some of the home-schoolers have cheated. Maybe some did, but I'm definitely planning a few lessons on accurate measuring, when we get back to normal!

Too tired for any more upcycling this weekend. I'm looking forward to relaxing in the garden with a glass of wine placed upon my 'new' garden coffee table! Enjoy yourselves too.

Love Amy xxx

Hello everyone,

Many thanks for all your get well messages – they really cheered me up. I'm just about recovered now. My flu was horrible, so goodness knows how awful the Corona virus must be. And those reports of 'long Covid' – truly dreadful.

Anyway, James surprised me this week with a question which I hardly knew how to answer. I'd welcome your thoughts, dear friends.

His question was whether I preferred 'Jimmy Juice' or 'Jimmy Jacks'. I hardly had time to respond before he offered 'James Juniper'.

I was spared the agony of replying as Ben came down the stairs and told him to stick with 'Jimmy Smith' if 'James Smith' wasn't good enough.

I opened the front door as James protested that he needed something with more pazazz. I made my escape as Ben declared that the food should provide the necessary pazazz!

I drove to the office, shuddering as I recalled last night's offering of lamb and rhubarb pie served with savoy cabbage pan-fried with scallops and a rhubarb jus. Perhaps 'Jimmy Juniper' was needed after all…

I made straight for the coffee pot when I arrived in the office.

Boosted by my caffeine intake, I told my colleagues all about James' proposed name changes. One said that 'Jimmy Sparkle' was quite catchy, while another said that 'Jimmy Stardust' was even better. No, I'm not going to put these ideas to James.

My only appointment of the week was a viewing of an interesting property over three floors with a reasonable garden. With a little bit of imagination and work it could be the perfect family home for the viewers who I knew had three teenagers.

I welcomed the couple in but got only a curt nod from the husband. I thought we'd start at the top of the house and so I led the way up the stairs, saying that this was a magnificent property.

My potential clients made no reply, but I didn't worry as conversations when everyone is in a line on the stairs are often a bit awkward.

I encouraged them to look out of the top window at what was surely the best view of the river that anyone could find anywhere in town.

Neither visitor came to look which was a pity as it truly was a great view.

Only then did they actually speak, telling me that their bottom line wouldn't depend on a pointless view and they weren't interested in anything outside their properties.

Well, that was a new one on me, but I said nothing. They were entitled to their opinion, so I carefully arranged my face into a smile.

My hopes diminished even further as we toured the rest of the house. None of my comments seemed to be going down well. The husband made heaps of notes as we went round but neither he nor his wife said much at all until we returned to the front door.

And then the woman announced that the house was clearly not worth anywhere near its asking price of £486,000 but they would take it off our hands for £135 K.

I couldn't hide my shock but the viewers were quick to explain.

They said that this would be their third development, so they knew the market. They would knock down the two bathrooms, giving them the extra space to re-configure the layout. All five of the bedrooms would get an en-suite and the living room would be converted into another en-suite bedroom. So the cost of six bathrooms needed to be deducted from the ridiculously high asking price, along with the expense of knocking the kitchen and dining rooms into one large open-plan space for the students to gather and relax in. Six fridges would be needed plus bi-fold doors leading into the garden.

Desperately I tried to inject some sanity into the proceedings, declaring that some of the updating expenses would usually be met by the purchasers. Some necessary works might be deducted but not all. And surely fewer fridges would be required – the tenants could take a shelf or two each in perhaps two fridges between them, I ventured bravely, not quite sure why I was even participating in this nonsense.

Of course this couple were not convinced, quite determined that their Homes of Multiple Occupancy simply exude luxury. Their profit margin depends on their de-luxe HMO model getting them top rents for the least outlay, they explained condescendingly.

What could I say? I am only the agent after alt. So I agreed to put their offer to the vendor, although I was fairly certain what the seller's response would be.

This odious couple didn't utter another word as they left, just dismissed me with another of the man's curt nods. I climbed wearily into my car and drove back to the viewer-free haven of the office.

My colleague, Gloria, took one look at my face and didn't bother asking how it had gone. She poured me a coffee and reached for the biscuit tin, saying, "Oh dear, one of those, was it?"

I nodded, shrugged and grimaced all at the same time. We estate agents are masters of multi-tasking.

Four biscuits later, I felt refreshed enough to make the phone call to the vendor. The conversation went pretty much as I'd expected. I got a distinctly unprofessional but satisfying pleasure out of conveying the news of rejection to the viewers.

I hope your day has gone well. Stay safe,
Love to you all, Justine x

Greetings to you all,

Hopefully, you won't all regret your praise for my poems as I present you with this week's offering!

Hope

Is our self-isolation
Imposed incarceration?
Sink not into anxiety

Is our social distancing
Enforced abandoning?
Fall not into melancholy

In troubled times, the sun still shines
Do not fret
In trying times, the wind still blows
Do not worry

In testing times, the rain still falls
Do not fear
In tormented times, children still play
Do not grieve

In torturous times, the world still turns
Do not despair

Flags of hope flutter yet

That's it – my 'Corona Anthology' is complete – you'll be relieved to hear!

Love to you all, Raquel x

Hello to all you dear ladies,

My visits to the park are slowly reviving my spirits. I love being in the open air again, right in the middle of all the nature which has been there all along, of course. Often arriving deliberately early, I love to sit quite still, drinking in all the sounds around me, sounds I might have dismissed once. Now I relish the rustle of leaves in the breeze, the calls of various birds, the buzzing of insects and the barking of excited dogs as they chase a ball or find a perfect stick. I particularly love hearing children playing and I'm surprising myself by enjoying the sounds of running feet and bicycles whizzing by.

I'm delighted to report that I've found a new sense of appreciation of the different trees and plants in the park and I make a point of brushing against the lavender bushes to release their sweet scents. I note with pleasure how various leaves are turning all the gorgeous yellows, oranges, reds and browns as autumn approaches. Once I even scooped up handfuls of fallen leaves and scattered them to the wind, enjoying the crispy feel of them as they settled around me like giant confetti.

I adore seeing all the living creatures around us: the birds, squirrels, insects and other people's dogs scampering about the grounds. It was a cause for celebration when I caught a rare glimpse of a hedgehog. Sometimes I even buy bread at the corner shop specifically to feed the ducks in the lake.

And I love sharing the municipal grounds with the human visitors, from the joggers to the dog owners to the young lady with her baby and toddler, Alec. I'm re-learning to greet them all in different ways: waving or nodding at some; exchanging smiles or greetings with others. Everyone keeps their distance, of course, yet still I relish the companionship of them all.

But most of all, I love my new friend, Carol, and look forward to being one half of a pair of beautiful, human bookends on a bench in the park.

Thanks for reading

Esther

Hello friends,

I've been racking my brain all week – what can I upcycle the old toilet into? My class have helped and they had some good ideas ranging from a seat to a bird bath to a fountain. One bright spark suggested that I should turn it into a planter and we all decided that this would work.

I cycled home yesterday and went into the garden to select the best position for the 'new' planter and got a big shock – the toilet was gone!

I wondered who on Earth would be so mad as to steal an old toilet! However, the culprit turned out to be my own dear husband!

Can you believe this? He had taken it to the council tip – he said that the bath and sink were terrible but bearable; however he was absolutely putting his foot down over the toilet. And my mother agreed with him, adding that we'd be the laughing stock of the whole neighbourhood! What do you all think?

I had to have an extra-large glass of wine and a chocolate muffin to get over it!

Hoping you are all well, Amy xxx

Greetings to you all,

Thank you very much for your encouraging words for my third poem – it's my last one. I'm hanging up my poetic pen now!

This week the twins' home-schooling project has been on researching and making a presentation about either of the Polar regions and its flora and fauna. At first I was so pleased because I naturally thought that they could do a region each and cover both Poles. Oh no, not my little horrors. They argued about who would do which and both wanted to do the South Pole. (Mostly because of that fabulous documentary on penguins – did you see it?) In the end we had to flip a coin for it and I really had to insist that the result was binding!

So Daisy got the North Pole and Arthur got his beloved penguins. They started work but were soon fighting over whether polar bears are better than penguins… AARGH! Not for the first time, I thought longingly of sending them back to school again…

But I said a while back that we must look for something positive every day (I must confess that I sometimes forget all about it). Well, today's positive is their impressive presentations. They have truly done so well and I'm so proud of them. Children are naturally so much better with technology than adults, don't you think? My dad always jokes that he needs the twins to help him program the TV recorder!

Love to you all, Raquel x

Hello fantastic friends,

Isn't the news fabulous – it seems almost impossible to imagine but lockdown is finally being eased here from next week. Hooray!!!

Hopefully, now that we will all be out of lockdown restrictions, we can arrange a get-together at last. A real party – what do you think, ladies? You could all come here and we'll make it a garden party. You can also see my upcycling, that way.

And I have a confession to make – I have upcycled one last shiny, red item. So I have a lovely, 'new' garden feature – can you guess what it is?

Well, I visited the garden centre and was pleased to find two plastic planters with a basket weave design. I've attached one to the handlebars and the other over the rear wheel of my shiny, red bike. My mother filled the baskets with petunias and trailing lobelia, which look so pretty.

The whole family agrees that my bicycle garden planter is my most successful upcycle ever. And it's also my last – sadly, I don't think that I'm really cut out for cycling or upcycling. I have some good ideas – well, I think so, anyhow! – but my skills are sadly lacking!

Must dash as we are all going out for a drive – my dusty, dear old car is in dire need of a good run before it goes back into normal service next week!

Have a wonderful week and let me know what dates suit you best for my party. I'm really looking forward to seeing you all soon.

Lots of love, Amy xxx

Dear Amy and friends,

Yes, the news about the end of lockdown is indeed wonderful. And I'm so excited to be invited to your party, Amy. I can hardly wait to meet you all in person and I just know that we'll have a marvellous time. Even though I haven't yet met most of you, we are all such good friends already!

I'm off for a little stroll now and I'm even contemplating leaving my mask in my pocket. Progress indeed!

Looking forward to seeing you all soon,

Love from Lois xxx

Hello everyone,

Such fantastic news to hear that you will all be out of lockdown next week. Yes, Amy, a garden party sounds <u>fantastic</u> and I'm dying to see your upcycling. Ben is most intrigued by your new bicycle garden feature! Our island's authorities are still keeping our borders restricted but I'll be booking our flights to visit you all as soon as I can.

Business is so slow here that I've only had one appointment this week. So I put on my best smile when I lifted the gleaming brass door knocker of the property I was due to value. The door was opened promptly by the homeowner, so promptly in fact that I think she must have been waiting in the hall for me. I was doubly glad that I always take care to be punctual.

The lady offered me a cup of tea and I knew right away that she was a real sweetie. Offers of refreshment are not often forthcoming! She served tea from a pretty china teapot decorated with tiny, purple flowers. The tea tray was beautifully set out with matching milk jug, sugar bowl, teacups and saucers and a little plate of dainty, home-made lemon biscuits. Impressive and so thoughtful!

Over our tea, I told this lovely, old lady that my Gran always said that tea tastes better from a teapot. She laughed and said that her grandmother would agree. The conversation flowed quite naturally onto our families and the lady chuckled as I told her all about my son James, or 'Jimmy Jacks' or whatever new name he was now pondering on.

In return, she told me about her two daughters and I admired some photos of her bonny grandchildren. This lovely lady explained that she was selling her bungalow to move in with her youngest daughter. I commiserated with her about the loss of her husband a year ago.

However, the woman wasn't at all downhearted, declaring herself to be very lucky to have a wonderful family. She was looking forward to seeing more of them and helping her daughter with her new baby.

I admired her cheerful, positive attitude – so refreshing. As I wandered through her immaculate home, I was also thinking about our list of home seekers. We have a couple who are looking for a two-bedroomed bungalow just like this one. If the lady decided to place her property on our books, this couple would be the first potential buyers that I would call.

I gave her my valuation of £299,000 and told her that she would be able to accept offers quite close to that figure as bungalows are rarely built nowadays and are much sought after.

And this wonderful woman was so happy, because she had no idea that it would be as much as that. Bless her, this lovely lady had made my day – no, she had made my week!

We soon had all the necessary paperwork in place and I left her property with a spring in my step.

Back at the office, I rang the couple who I thought would love this bungalow and set up a viewing for tomorrow. I have a good feeling about this one.

When I arrived home this afternoon, I could hear Ben and James laughing together. They were discussing possible names again and debating over 'Jumping Jimmy Jacks' and 'James Flames' – can you imagine anything worse? I'll have a quiet word with James later – wish me luck.

Hope you are all having a great week and I look forward to seeing you in person soon,

Love to everyone, Justine x

Hello dearest ladies,

Finally we're to come out of lockdown here – I think that's worthy of a loud cheer and at least three exclamation marks!!!

I'm so looking forward to the party and getting to meet you all at last. I agree totally with Lois: we'll have so much to discuss as we're all such marvellous friends already. Thanks for all your kind messages inviting Carol to join our celebration – she's delighted to be included and also so happy to have a party to look forward to (that seems quite ungrammatical but today is too exciting to worry about it).

I know I'm repeating things, but I'm so looking forward to seeing you at the party very soon.

Thanks for reading,

Esther

Greetings to you all,

Freedom from lockdown at last – yippee! My kids are overjoyed to be back at school – I'd never have thought that possible! We made their first day back extra-special by going to our favourite café for tea: bacon sandwiches for the twins and beans on toast for me. It was absolute heaven to be out again!

Arthur and Daisy are so excited about the party. They can't wait to meet up with Julie & Mark, and also with great-aunty Esther. I'm thrilled to be meeting up with every single one of you! (Plus Andy & Ben, of course). So here's an extra cheer for the 21st of next month – and thanks again to Amy for organising our celebrations. Plenty of 'fizz' on ice for us grown-ups!

Love to you all, Raquel x